I0741939

This book is dedicated to my three beautiful children Nyrie, Nylah, and Nyaire.
May the LORD continue to bless you with whatever your heart's desire.

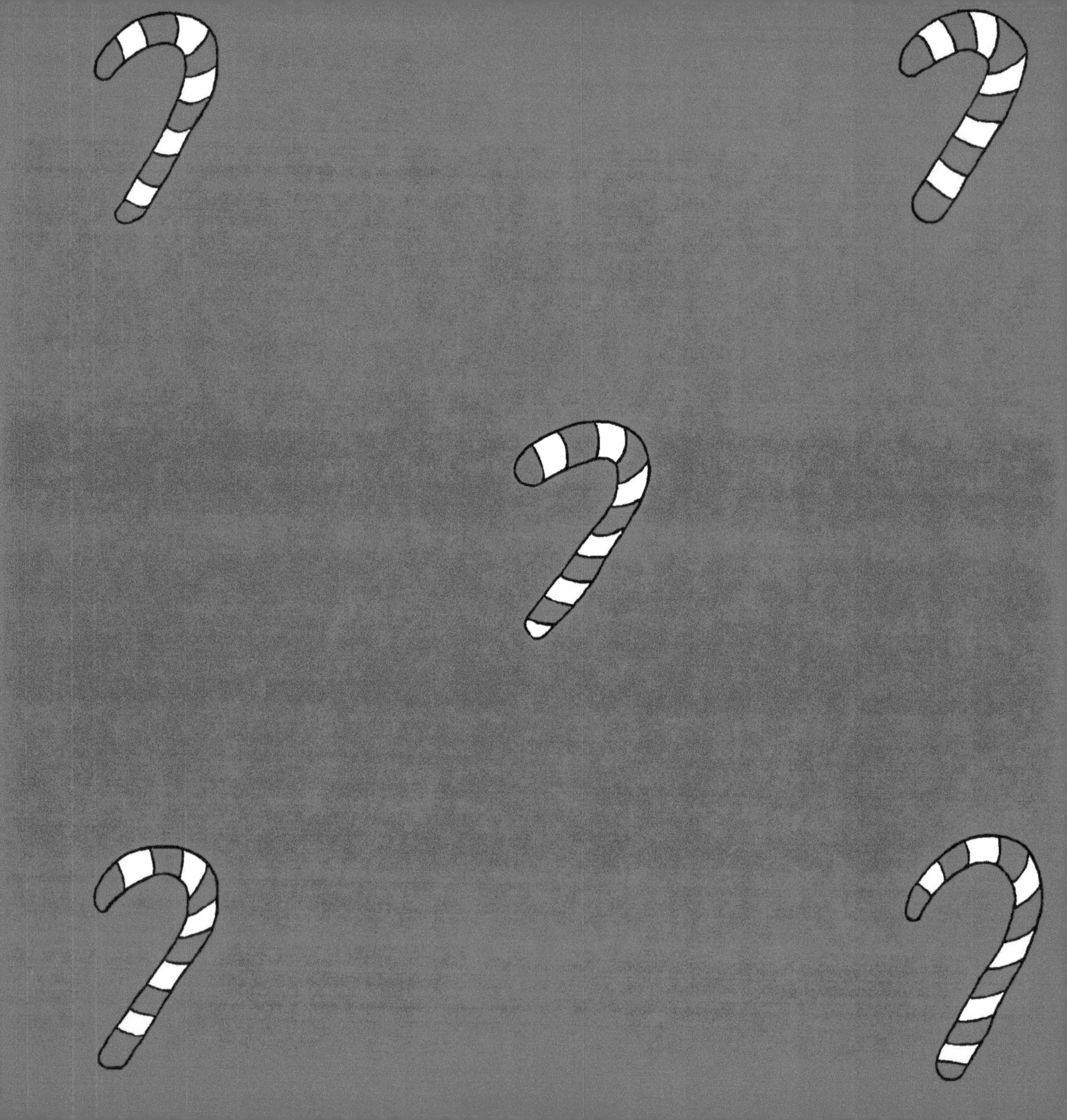

What I Love About Christmas

I love the smell of sweet roasted peanuts, cinnamon and pine trees. The love that fills the air and takes your mind off the cool breeze.

Christmas Tree Farm
Daruti's Bakery
$$$
HOT ROASTED PEANUTS
PEANUTS

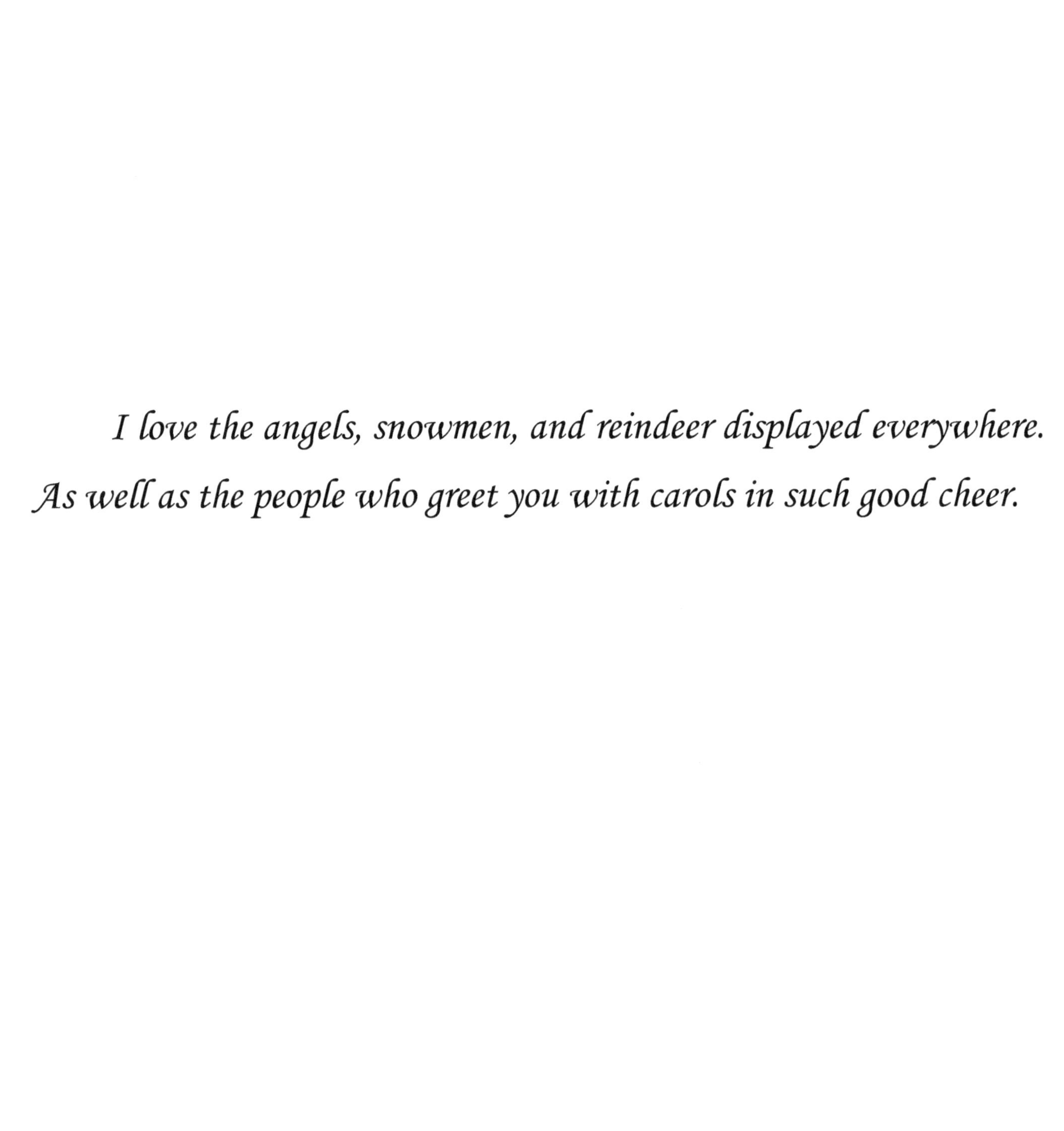

I love the angels, snowmen, and reindeer displayed everywhere.

As well as the people who greet you with carols in such good cheer.

I love the time we have off to get some extra zzz's. Then, we wake up to a beautiful surprise; the thick layers of snow covering the houses and the trees.

I love to see all of the children nicely dressed and lined up with their Christmas lists. All to take a picture and share their secrets with good old St. Nick.

On Christmas night, I love to see all of the decorations come together with the assorted lights; Oh what a sight!

I love exchanging gifts that come from the heart. Then taking a nap in the scattered wrapping paper we tore apart.

I love when the family gathers at the table before we eat to pray. We give thanks for our union and the real reason we celebrate this day. We thank the LORD for allowing us to spend this day together; that's to say the least. Then we sit down and stuff our faces and enjoy our great big feast.

After dinner has been eaten and the family parts; we sit and reminisce about every moment that puts joy in our hearts.

Before we go to sleep we say a prayer by the window to the brightest starlight. Then end it with many blessings to all. We love you. Goodnight.